A Cold Winter's Good Knight

Shelley Moore Thomas ☾ PICTURES BY **Jennifer Plecas**

Dutton Children's Books

DUTTON CHILDREN'S BOOKS
A division of Penguin Young Readers Group

Published by the Penguin Group
Penguin Group (USA) Inc., 375 Hudson Street, New York, New York 10014, U.S.A.
Penguin Group (Canada), 90 Eglinton Avenue East, Suite 700, Toronto, Ontario, Canada M4P 2Y3 (a division
of Pearson Penguin Canada Inc.) • Penguin Books Ltd, 80 Strand, London WC2R 0RL, England • Penguin Ireland,
25 St Stephen's Green, Dublin 2, Ireland (a division of Penguin Books Ltd) • Penguin Group (Australia), 250 Camberwell
Road, Camberwell, Victoria 3124, Australia (a division of Pearson Australia Group Pty Ltd) • Penguin Books India Pvt Ltd,
11 Community Centre, Panchsheel Park, New Delhi - 110 017, India • Penguin Group (NZ), 67 Apollo Drive, Rosedale,
North Shore 0632, New Zealand (a division of Pearson New Zealand Ltd) • Penguin Books (South Africa) (Pty) Ltd,
24 Sturdee Avenue, Rosebank, Johannesburg 2196, South Africa Penguin Books Ltd, Registered Offices:
80 Strand, London WC2R 0RL, England

LIBRARY OF CONGRESS CATALOGING-IN-PUBLICATION DATA

Thomas, Shelley Moore.
A cold winter's Good Knight / by Shelley Moore Thomas; illustrated by Jennifer Plecas.
p. cm.
Summary: When three little dragons come to the castle on the night of
a fancy ball, the Good Knight must remind them to mind their manners.
ISBN 978-0-525-47964-2 (hardcover)
[1. Dragons—Fiction. 2. Behavior—Fiction. 3. Etiquette—Fiction.]
I. Plecas, Jennifer, ill. II. Title.
PZ7.T369453Co 2008   [E]—dc22   2007048523

Published in the United States by Dutton Children's Books,
a division of Penguin Young Readers Group
345 Hudson Street, New York, New York 10014
www.penguin.com/youngreaders

Designed by Sara Reynolds and Abby Kuperstock
Manufactured in China   First Edition
4 6 8 10 9 7 5 3

For Issy

S.M.T.

For Rosanne, my couz

J.P.

It was a cold winter's night in the king's forest. A big storm had dumped lots and lots of freezing snow on top of a tiny cave.

Three little dragons sat inside. They were shivering.

"Brrrrrr," they said.

"I am colder than a snowball,"
said the first dragon.

"I am colder than an ice cube,"
said the second dragon.

"I am colder than a popsicle,"
said the third dragon.

The dragons' teeth were chattering so loudly that the
Good Knight heard the noise all the way at the king's castle.
So the Good Knight got on his horse and rode clippety-clop
to the dragons' cave.

"Never fear, my dragon friends," he said. "It is warm in the
king's castle. Come with me. Methinks you will be toasty and
cozy there."

"Yippee!" said the dragons as they climbed into the sled.

"But there is one thing I must tell you," said the Good Knight. "There is a ball at the castle tonight. You must mind your manners."

"Oh, we will," said the dragons.

The Good Knight's horse trudged through the thick, wet snow. Clippety-slop. Clippety-slop.

When they came near the castle, it looked very fancy and festive. It also looked very warm!

Inside, fires were burning in every fireplace. Candles were glowing by every window. Musicians were playing. Guests were dancing.

"Dragons," said the Good Knight, "I told you this was a fancy ball. So use good manners. Stay here by the fireplace, and stay out of trouble."

"Oh, we will," the little dragons said.

But dragons will be dragons.

"I am still cold," said the first dragon.

"The fire could be warmer," said the second dragon.

"Let's blow on it," said the third dragon.

The little dragons started blowing their fiery breath on the fire to warm it up. The flames grew.

"Awesome," said all three dragons. "We are nice and warm now."

But the guests at the ball did not like the bigger fire. Smoke came pouring out of the fireplace.

The Good Knight ran back to the dragons. "Put that fire out right now, dragons," commanded the Good Knight.

The dragons grabbed the punch bowl.

The fire was soaked. So was the Good Knight.

"Oops," said the dragons. "We're sorry."

"Now, dragons," said the Good Knight. "Stay here on the stairs, and remember, mind your manners."

"Oh, we will," said the dragons.

The Good Knight went back to his post at the door.

But dragons will be dragons.

"Look," said the first dragon.
He pointed to the glowing chandelier.

"Oooohh,"
said the second dragon.

"What a great swing,"
cried the third dragon.

The dragons leaped from the stairs onto the chandelier and swung across the room.

COWABUNGA!

YIPPEE!

YAHOO!

The chandelier swung from side to side. The guests below gasped.

Just then the Good Knight showed up.

"Come down right now, dragons," commanded the Good Knight.

Down came the dragons . . . and the chandelier!

"Oops," said the dragons. "We're sorry."

"Dragons!" said the Good Knight, "I told you this was
a fancy ball. Now stay here by the table. And mind your
manners."

"Oh, we will," said the dragons.

But dragons will be dragons.

The first dragon pointed to the cake.
"I am hungry," he said.

The second dragon pointed to the musicians.
"I want to play that harp," she said.

The third dragon jumped up and down.
"I want to dance with a princess!" he cried.

But this time the Good Knight had been watching the dragons.

DON'T EVEN THINK ABOUT IT!

He raced across the room to protect the cake, the harp, and the princess.

"You three dragons are ruining the king's ball. Why aren't you using your manners?" cried the Good Knight.

The little dragons hung their heads.

"What *are* manners?" they asked.

"Good grief," said the Good Knight.

He bent down and whispered, "Manners mean being polite. Manners mean saying please and thank you. And most of all manners mean thinking before you do something."

"Oh," said all three dragons. "We are sorry. We did not mean to ruin the ball."

They sat and thought for a long time. They felt truly awful about their wild behavior.

"Maybe we should try manners," said the first dragon.

"May I have a piece of cake. . . . Please?"
the little dragon asked the cook.

"Thank you," said the dragon.

"May I look at your harp. . . . Please?"
the second dragon asked the minstrel.

please?

Thank
you!

"Thank you," said the dragon.

"May I have the honor of this dance. . . . Please?"
the third dragon asked the princess.
She nodded.

"Thank you," said the dragon.

And so, 'twas the use of good manners that saved the king's ball. The king's guests were now happy, one and all,

especially the Good Knight!